The soul becomes dyed with the color of its thoughts

Marcus Aurelius

Henry Funk

The Third King

A Short Story of Culture Clash

Bibliografische Information der Deutschen Nationalbibliothek:
Die Deutsche Nationalbibliothek verzeichnet diese Publikation in der Deutschen Nationalbibliografie; detaillierte bibliografische Daten sind im Internet über http://dnb.dnb.de abrufbar.

Editor: Erica K. Freeman, Philadelphia PA

Translation from the German: Timo Piecha
Cover: Timo Piecha

Photo: Donnie Fenell 1972

Herstellung und Verlag: BoD – Books on Demand, Norderstedt

ISBN: 9783757809591

Dedicated to US Army Specialist Donnie Fenell and to all of those who suffered a similar dose of culture shock.

I

In front of a traffic light, right beneath the gate to Fiori Kaserne, the engine of a vintage convertible could be heard. It was a shiny "Isabella" whose cream color made the classic car seem to vanish in the driven snow.

"You should have known," the driver mumbled to herself. "Yes, Gesine, this you should have known."

Dense layers of snow slowly covered the war machinery lined up under the motor pool lanterns. Gusty winds whipped the few uniformed men unlucky enough to be outdoors back into the shelter of the building blocks.

A furious whirlwind fed by fat flakes kept growing in the center of the intersection and made her dizzy. No matter how carefully Gesine's feet moved the pedals, the tires could not get a grip on the slippery winter road. Behind her, another car's horn started to blow. Lively waving from the driver indicated she had better get into gear and get going.

She must have appeared to him like a fish behind milky glass as she repeated her words like a pantomime.

"Sixty! Two! Sixty-two years, yes! Dammit!" Her driver's license was years older than most of the buggers lined up behind her, bullying her with their flashing headlights and blowing horns. Abruptly, the light changed to red. Gesine unbuttoned her loden coat, lifted her chin. As she freed herself from her woolen scarf, which she stuffed under her thighs for safe keeping, she stared at the street.

"You just had to take the Isabella," she admonished herself again. The convertible was really only meant to be driven during the summer. And if it had not been for Justus letting her down, the car would have remained in the garage until far into late spring.

"You could've taken a cab," she mumbled.

Green. In spite of the hurry she was in, she forced herself to stay calm. She sucked on her lower lip and concentrated on the interaction between the pedals under her feet. The Isabella fishtailed slightly, moving up the Schweinheim Heights.

Gesine turned into Rhoenstrasse, finding the NCO Club to her left. She carefully applied the brakes, however, determined to cross the street without any hesitation as soon as the oncoming traffic had passed her. No more unnecessary stopping, she told herself.

A line of military vehicles approached from the direction of Ready Barracks. Mighty cones of light blinded her. A passing plow deposited a thick layer of muddy snow over the Isabella's hood as the street beneath began shaking. The steering wheel and seat vibrated. Less than a step away from her, one of three combat tanks passed. The clanging of the chains made her cover her ears. The barking of blackened exhaust pipes made her shudder. Caught in a mist of soot, Gesine was awaiting the end of this creepy parade.

Which one of the two levers was for wiping the windshield? She chose the left one—no, both—with both hands. The wipers threatened to fail, shaking and squeaking. Finally they presented a vision of pure darkness. In her anxiety, switching and pulling, Gesine had turned off the headlights. She drove the car onto the NCO Club's parking lot, which reminded her of a snow-covered, frozen lake, laying immaculately in the midst of the turmoil. The snowfall ceased. Clouds broke open, and a pale disc appeared in the open sky. Stars flickering, the universe gained in depth.

"Some of them aren't there anymore," she thought. "Just beams of light, on their way to us. We see what is no more."

Her heart was still racing, and she tried to calm it by slowing the rhythm of her breathing.

"You couldn't have known that would happen, Gesine."

All this trouble because of Justus, who had let her down. Woe to him if they didn't have an officer for her in store anymore!

The soft light of the moon sufficed to illuminate her face in the rearview mirror—her rouge had suffered a little. She grabbed her handbag from the passenger seat and found a compact. Around the eyes all efforts would be in vain. Deeply withdrawn into the hollows, they left deep furrows, that couldn't be masked. Her cheeks, whose overly tight skin she powdered with a strawberry-pink shade, were lacking fullness. Lipstick she applied hesitantly. For its simple use she perceived as frivolous—however it did help soften the wrinkles around her aged mouth, which looked like it was wearing a zipper.

She was confident that she would be presented a young officer that would meet her expectations, since she had clearly stressed her wishes to the young lady of the public affairs office by speaking to her on the phone beforehand. A young man of good upbringing, a nice college boy—that was what she was prepared for. Although as a widow of a late city councilman her name no longer appeared on the official US Community Commander guest list, the woman from the PAO had remembered Gesine very well to be one of the leading figures in the local German community. Gesine had always been the first one to receive an invitation to tea with the commander's wife. At any official function, she and her husband had been routinely placed next to established families of beer brewers. The chief of police was always seated across from them. Representatives of the Chambers of Commerce were considered last.

Gesine could have had the officer delivered directly to her house if she had so desired, but a visit with the Americans felt right to her now that she made fewer public appearances since her husband's death. Too much silence in her old age—that is what she feared most.

She switched off the engine. Grabbing the door frame, she lifted herself from the seat and freeing the scarf from under her thighs. Her foot slipped forward, and she tumbled out of the car with elbows and buttocks thudding the ground. A sting of pain drove into her pelvis.

"The hips, for God's sake, not the hips!"

She looked towards the entrance of the NCO Club, which threatened to fade from her sight. Nothing moved. According to the number of cars parked out front, there must have been at least twenty people in the building, fostering good German-American relations.

Cold crept into her bones, and frost numbed her backside. She had to get up. From the street afar no one could see her lying behind her car. In front of her, nothing but the snow-powdered parking lot.

On the other side of the lot, she noticed the silhouette of a person, who began to trot towards her. The contours revealed those of a tall man, the clouds of his steaming breath increasing with each of his steps. But what was wrong with his head? So big, so round! A globe-like ball, whose shadow slipped between Gesine's face and the night sky, producing a fine shine around what she now recognized to be a mass of curly hair.

He's black, she mused, of the friendly kind I hope.

„Are you hurt? Let me help you up, madam," she heard the shadow say.

* * *

II

"My name is Rufus Moody, Junior. Yeesh ..."

Rufus had two hours left to learn his formal greeting by heart. He placed the instruction leaflet for soldiers visiting with German families on top of the perfectly folded blanket that covered his bunk. He opened his locker to grab soap and a towel.

"American Forces Radio!" Wolfman Jack's voice was cawing from the battery-powered transistor by the window as he introduced the theme from the new movie Superfly. In the center of the room, four soldiers sat around a table and a bottle of Wild Turkey. Stacks of dollar bills were placed next to each of the players. Three black guys and one who looked somewhat like a Latino were arguing over a game of Blackjack.

Moody's roommate, a chubby giant named Private Clarence F. Jackson, had gambled himself into a serious problem.

Gonzalez folded his cards. "Puta madre! Dis look like trouble."

Williams, otherwise called "The Dog," raised his hands in the air while heading for the door. "I'm out. This dude screwed up—big time."

Jackson and Winslow stayed in their seats eyeing each other. Winslow chewed a toothpick, holding the ten of diamonds between two fingers.

You would've been burnt, Jackson."

"It must have slipped ..."

"No, man, you would have been burnt. Game over—you owe."

Jackson's massive body started shaking as he babbled promises of redemption. Winslow fell quiet, helped himself to his opponent's pack of Kools, lit one, and inhaled all the way to the bottom of his lungs. A deep sigh of boredom followed, as he plucked crumbs of dried ointment from his beard. Winslow mumbled along to the melody that was flowing from the radio: "Freddie's dead, that's what I said ..."

Moody knew what came next. Winslow would talk Jackson into some kind of dirty deal that would get the miserable soldier even deeper in dept. Winslow had a bunch of guys in the unit under his thumb. Gambling debts. Whenever somebody dared to start trouble with him, two or three of his debtors backed him up. Winslow, the loan shark, had the final say.

Moody ignored Jackson's puppy-eyed look. With a towel around his hips and his Class A uniform on a dress hanger, he headed for the shower room down the hall, thinking that there was no point in messing around with Winslow. Jackson, you a jerk!

Moody pictured the falling snow outside as he let the hot water run over his body. In two more hours he'd be facing the greatest adventure since enlisting. What will her house look like? What will they talk about? He held his open mouth under the stream of water and swallowed against the dryness that crept up in his mouth like a filthy tennis ball. This thing, this lump, this uncontrollable feeling was called doubt. Maybe he wouldn't be as welcome as he'd been promised. But hadn't she been there to pick up an American? Yes, Moody, an American, he thought. But a black one?

A lieutenant Flannegan from Headquarters Company had been selected and had been waiting for the older woman inside the club. What a fine specimen of a soldier he was: blonde and tanned, with an open smile. It was only lethargy of his southern tongue that spoiled that almost perfect picture of a sporty young character.

But Moody? Had he only been accepted because he had found her lying helpless in the snow? Leaning on his shoulder as he helped her into the NCO Club, had she merely felt obligated to include him in the pairings of American soldiers with German families? She had looked somewhat clueless after the young woman from the public affairs office had thanked Rufus for rescuing Mrs. Gesine Diefenbach—not daring to imagine the scandal it might have caused, had they found her deep-frozen on a military parking lot.

Anticipating the dilemma, Gesine had spoken up in a sharp British sounding accent, "I will take him." Moody considered her offer with great unease, just as generations of ancestors had done before him when a white person had laid claim to them.

Moody grabbed the towel, dried his skin, and started to dress. „Man! She can't just take me, can she?" he thought wondering.

He ought to be happy; the PAO-woman had congratulated him for being chosen for the Christmas program since only outstanding soldiers were selected for this privilege. A bit stiff, she had then turned to the older woman, saying with assurance, "Both will be on time."

* * *

III

The table had suffered two broken legs. Its top sloped upwardly into the room. Jackson leaned against it, with a swelling cut above his right eyebrow. Moody handed his wet towel and told him to cover the wound. Upon closer examination the injury proved to be less dangerous than expected at first sight.

"Noth'n but a warning," Jackson sought to explain. "Ain't noth'n to it. Can't reason with the pusher man ..."

"You're a fuckin' jerk, man!" Moody didn't want to have anything to do with Jackson's troubles. Yet he gave in as Jackson begged a fat number of greenbacks off him to settle his debts with Winslow. Jackson might have passed as mentally deficient, but this was no reason to leave him as easy prey for Winslow. Moody checked his wallet and counted the bills.

"That should do. I'll go pay him."

"Thanks, brother, right on. You can count on me anytime, bro." Jackson bathed in excessive deference.

"Never mind, Jackson, never mind. Just pay me back, okay?"

Moody was running out of time; only half an hour was left before he was expected by the gate. He stepped into the hallway and followed the music roaring from a room five doors down called The Bunker. He was forbidden to enter since he did not belong to the band of Vietnam vets, to this group of men, whose screams echoed through the barracks at night—men, who drowned their nightmares in booze or misted the rising memories with clouds of dope.

Rufus yielded for a moment. As he stood there, his thoughts returned to his home, reminding him of his Uncle Sylvester, who had suffered the same way these guys did. Uncle Sly, whose wounds were caused by a war most of them were forced to enter, had an ugly scar on his heart.

Ever since his Army discharge, Uncle Sly's radius of life had been reduced to a path from his bed to the porch and back again—only to return later, back into the sun, where he'd sit, motionless as a reptile in the heat of the day, mouth hanging open. Sly's routine grip on the bourbon bottle was accompanied by facial convulsions, shifting between a grin and a look of melancholic yearning. And as if the uncle had to reassure himself of his salvation, he constantly caressed his snakeskin boot in which an iron prosthesis replaced his right foot. It was payment for his participation in the suffering he had brought to innocent people, whose faces still haunted him.

But time was captured in a permanently repeating sequence: they had been on a recon patrol in an area declared as clear of enemy forces when the impenetrable green started to spit machine gun fire. Sly jumped for shelter and drowned in a sea of pain. Spears of bamboo, knee-high, sliced his combat boots and bore through the soles of his feet, nailing him like Jesus to the cross. And the rain seemed to never end.

Caught in solitude he began to pray out loud. And when the pain was about to drive him insane he cursed the land of those communist heathens, thundering so the birds were terrified in the trees.

"Fuck, I'm stuck!" These words had never been more suitable as during these endless hours. And as his fever dared to weaken him, the Lord sent him the serpent. A tiger python, longer than a man's height, had sensed the heat of the fevering human body.

It slid into the pit to embrace the rump of the impaled man with breathtaking speed. One was to become the other's victim. Uncle Sly's waning powers still sufficed to break a lance from the wooden spears surrounding him and thrust it into the python's throat. The pharyngeal reflex slowly died. And while the gangrene consumed the burning flesh off his feet, the python kept him alive—slice by slice. And when finally there was only the snakeskin left, Sly twined the trophy around his neck, ready to succumb.

Uncounted monsoon-days later the inscrutably smiling soldier was rescued and flown out. Dispatched onto his front porch, so Sly claimed to remember. The Purple Heart affixed to his sleeve, he had not left the porch ever since. It seemed impossible to cross the heaving sea of bamboo spikes covering the front yard.

Sly, way back home in Louisiana and those veterans behind the door to The Bunker belonged to a generation of men, who withstood death yet lost the rest of their lives.

Moody pushed the door handle. No one paid attention to him as he entered this hole decorated with camouflage nets and filled with the bitter scent of any smokable drug. He recognized "The Dog" Williams wearing a black headband. Winslow sat on an ammu-nition box, his switchblade scoring fine lines into the skin of his forearm and letting himself being slapped by Jimi's guitar riffs —"Machine Gun". Struck down by a burst of Buddy Miles's drumfire, his body crumpled up.

Moody held a bundle of dollar bills in front of his face: "Leave Jackson alone. He's paid his dues."

Winslow looked at him with bloodshot eyes, a pitiful sight. At this very moment, Winslow could have been an easy victim for the devil that was riding him. However, Satan didn't seem to be finished with this poor creature.

"You're such a noble guy, Moody!" Winslow's hand padded over the table, searching until it found a joint the size of a two thumbs-long candle—they called it a "peacemaker": content unknown, effects unpredictable.

"Merry Christmas." As if to affix a medal onto Moody's chest, Winslow stuffed the gigantic joint into the breast pocket of Moody's shirt.

"They'll fall for you like flies, those Fräuleins. 'What a pretty little ‚negro' they'll say." Winslow pressed his blessing through a clenched row of teeth. "But beware, brother, that your soul doesn't suffer any damage out there. Amen. And now—get your ass outa here. Out!"

* * *

IV

"Lookin' sharp!" Jackson admired Private Rufus Moody, Jr. as he presented himself in his Class A uniform along with a paper bag filled with presents under his arm. Moody set his cap down into his carefully pressed hairdo. "Stay outta trouble, man."

"You too, man."

Dawn was already breaking. Moody slid over the icey cobblestones towards the Kaserne gate where Lieutenant Flannegan was expecting him, carrying an identical paper bag. Hair neatly parted, and spreading the scent of Old Spice aftershave, the officer kept his feet in motion. Patent leather shoes were not made for winter use. Moody saluted. "Good evening, sir!"

Flannegan answered the salute, obviously uncom-fortable. Would they really be able to pull this off?, he wondered. Both should at all times be aware that in uniform they were representing the United States Army.

I guess we'll work it out somehow, won't we, Moody?" Flannegan nudged him in his side, as if they were members of the same country club, comrades for ages. "Won't we? We won't embar-rass ourselves?"

The answer took time. Moody was distracted by a group of black men passing by in fur coats and wide, colorful hats, eyeing him suspiciously.

"Have fun, Uncle Tom," he heard one of them say.

Moody did not like these braggarts, acting like they were dangerous, cool, some of them quick with the switch blade. Nobody forced them to be here. There was no more draft, their stay was voluntary, except for some of the dealers, pimps, and minor criminals, who'd been given the choice between jail or military service.

"We won't embarrass ourselves, will we?" Flannegan said again.

We? Moody thought. Us? Aside from the fact they were waiting to be picked up, the two men had very little in common. Like beef steak and pig feet, he thought and smiled silently. Back home they would even go to different churches, where they would hear the same words but from different mouths and for different folks with different strokes.

"That's blood, isn't it?" Flannegan nervously pointed to the collar peeking out from beneath Moody's coat.

"Must come from the nosebleeds that catch me sometimes when I'm excited," Moody replied, cursing Jackson silently.

At that same moment a midnight-blue Mercedes limousine drove up. A young, fragile man with dark, long hair waved from behind the steering wheel. He wore wire-rimmed, John Lennon glasses, and upon closer examination a thin beard could be noticed around his chin. Instinctively, Flannegan opened the door to the front passenger's seat. "If you screw up, Moody, I'll kick your ass, I swear," he whispered before entering the vehicle.

The chauffeur introduced himself as Justus, their host's grandson. His English sounded acceptable, but with a distinctly German accent: "Zizz izz se way to my grandmahzzer's house."

From the backseat to which he was exiled, Moody watched the driver, who didn't let the snow faze him. That fancy limousine (what a blast!) rushed down Würzburger Strasse, making a right turn in front of Jaeger Kaserne. After crossing two or three intersections, they turned uphill again into a gathering of impressive stone villas along one side. Across the street, a snow-covered path, marked by the yellow sprinkles of dogs' led to an underbrush of trees.

Leaning on a cane, the old woman, was waiting for them by the front door. Next to the stairs, Moody recognized the old-time convertible standing in a wide garage. Flannegan took the lead and his introduction sounded perfect, as far as Moody was able to judge. The woman reacted with excitement. The German greeting he had intended to perfect refused to come, so Moody just gave a simple, "Hello, Madam."

What a tree! As they took off their coats they were led to a simple, yet tastefully decorated fir, whose top almost touched the high ceiling. The needles produced a fresh scent that hung over the genuine upholstery and aged wooden furniture. A massive pair of stag's antlers hung over a stonecrafted fireplace and gave Flannegan the opportunity to bring the men of his family into the conversation, since they'd been hunters for generations. Over by a wide front of windows, a festive table was set for four, bearing fine silver, a massive candle holder, and porcelain dishes.

The host welcomed her guests and thanked Moody again for her rescue. An inaudible, aged maid offered a tray with small glasses filled with a doughy, yoke-like liquid.

"Try it!" the woman prodded. "It is homemade! When I was a child we made this from our own chickens. But when you are a wife of an important man, you don't have chickens anymore."

The stuff tasted horrible, especially since Moody always refrained from alcohol, having witnessed its effect on his father and his Uncle Sly.

"Aheerleekohr? Aha, very good," Moody politely replied, causing Justus to smile, and hand him a second one as a "warm-up." "Prost! Cheers!" Moody's empty stomach rebelled furiously.

They spent time reminiscing about the achievements of the woman's late husband, who for his entire life had worked for good German-American relations. The recognition of his efforts could be read on a fancy document framed over the fireplace. The former city councilman had been announced Honorary Colonel of the US Armored Battalion stationed in Ready Kaserne, calling themselves "The Tuskers."

"A Tusker! One of us," Flannegan remarked with appreciation.

The woman called her husband a man of high moral standards. She looked over the pictures from his younger years, which showed him wearing a black World War II uniform.

"During the great war he was a lieutenant like you," she told Flannegan who replied in the old-fashioned talk of the "Old South", saying, "Yes, ma'am, he sure was."

Moody politely declined a third glass and felt relieved when they were asked to join the table. The two guests were placed opposite each other so that both could sit next to their hostess. Moody was irritated by the table setting. He had never needed more than a fork and a knife at home. He and his father had kept it simple when it came to cooking. But here, bowls stood on smaller plates on bigger plates; everything seemed to be set up in doubles, even triples. And his information sheet for soldiers in German families did not say anything about German dining habits. He would take his cues from the others.

The maid tiptoed around the table and filled tall, thin glasses with champagne. Once again the guests were welcomed, toasts were spoken, and glasses were lifted. Before he had had the least bite to eat, Moody was filled up, toast by toast—first with liquor, then topped by German sparkling wine. And now a bowl of soup was to follow before the real dinner that he craved.

Their hostess's face had turned rosy while the hot consommé pulled sweat from his forehead.

"Where do you come from in America?" the old woman asked. "New York? Chicago?" Cities she had visited with her husband. "Green River, Georgia," Flannegan's rolling tongue revealed.

"And you, Rufus? May I call you Rufus?"

"Yes, madam, Rufus is okay. Versbach."

Justus and his grandmother sat baffled.

"Versbach, near Wuerzburg," Moody explained. Though raised in Louisiana, he was born in a small Franconian village not too far from the home of his host. Moody explained that in the mid-fifties his father, Rufus Moody, Sr., was stationed in Wuerzburg with the 3rd Infantry Division. During a visit to the Talavera Wine Festival, he met Gabi Endres. And the rest of the story is history, though not a simple one.

"Yes, it surely must have been not so simple", the woman agreed.

For a moment, his memory carried him back home, far back into his childhood—yet the image of his mother remained hidden. His father had banned any trace of her from their home, so Rufus wasn't sure whether his picture of her was a product of his fantasy or resembled any real memory. In this instant he realized that he had enlisted in the Army for only one reason—to come to Germany and search for that part of him he'd always felt had been missing. Sitting here at this table he took as a preparation, a rehearsal for the moment he longed for, making sure that he would not fail when they would meet each other again. Part of his master plan was to take a train to Wuerzburg. Not yet, not yet, fearing to lose her again by not proving worthy.

Justus's voice pulled him back into reality. "Such things still aren't easy today," the fragile grandson said, while setting the corkscrew to a bottle of what he called „Kroever Nacktarsch". To lighten the mood, he told Flannegan, "Mosel-wein," pointing at the label which showed a young boy getting his naked butt spanked. "Naked ass," he translated with a pointed smile. "I love „Nacktarsch"."

Moody figured at home nobody would give such a filthy name to a wine, least of all applying such a perverted label. The stuff tasted sour anyway.

"Prost! Riesling? Oh yes, very good." He wondered if he should ask the mute maid for a Coke.

The main course was rolled in on a serving trolley, on a tray hidden under a huge silver dome. Grandmother and grandson pretended to be utterly excited, until the secret was lifted and a steamed carp goggled at them. The sight made the Germans hum with delight, while the guests showed their surprise, silently lifting their eyebrows and signaling each other to be courageous. Motivated by her employer, the servant loaded the plates generously with chunks of fish fillet swam on each dish, accompanied by boiled, halved potatoes prepared in a light sauce and sprinkled with herbs before placing it on the table.

Justus had unscrewed the next bottle. With one hand he filled Flannegan's glass; the other one he laid on the lieutenant's shoulder. Another toast was made.

To this very moment, no one had interrupted the drinking with prayer. Moody wanted to thank the Lord at least silently, so he closed his eyes for a silent moment of devotion. Whether everything was alright with him, the hostess inquired. Moody nodded aimably and noticed the scent of the sauce was similar to that of the drink in his glass.

If one squashed the green, raisin-like berries with one's tongue, they released a salty-sour taste, mingling with the starchy sauce which glued the fish to one's palate, leaving no choice but to flush it down with the „Nacktarsch".

He could tell he was being observed. Yet he found nothing wrong with his manners, and the grumbling in his guts could not be so loud that it would raise attention. Still, he noticed that the old woman was checking him out, until he responded with a stare.

"The mother from Versbach..." she began, picking up her glass and smiling at Moody.

„Ich schwarz, du schwarz," she said.

Her statement caused irritation. Giggling she repeated: "Ich schwarz, du schwarz." Although the others were unable to follow her thoughts, she snorted with laughter and wiped the tears from her eyes.

Justus sent a prayer towards the sky and took the sting out of the joke by explaining. In Germany, political conservatives are considered as the Blacks whereas social democrats and further left winged were the Reds thus comparing her political stand with the appearance of her guest, thereby bursting out in approval, "I'm black, you're black!"

His burp could not be overheard. Moody apologized, short of breath, and obviously trying to keep the belch to himself. Within a second, Justus was on his way to the house bar calling, "Medicine! Medicine!" The content of the brown bottle he retreieved would be the best thing for the burning in his stomach, he advised Moody, who had been warned of the German Schnapps before he had taken off to Europe.

Well, but only one! The name of the booze seemed impossible to pronounce to Moody even though Justus was constantly repeating it, "Spessartraeuber! Down with it!"

The hostess escorted her guests to the glowing tree, where the maid struggled to light the candles at its top. Towering over her by at least two heads, Moody took the matches and completed the lighting. The maid noticed him marveling at the picture of the angel on the matchbox and signaled for him to keep it with a slight wave of her hand.

Meanwhile Justus had put on a record and let the needle sink into the grooves of the disc. Silent night, holy night. Velvety, mellow. The lady's facial features relaxed immediately.

"Harry Belafonte," she romanticized, "A negro, like you, dear Rufus. Homesick now? He sings so beautiful…"

He really appreciated this gesture, he replied, although he had never been exposed to Harry Belafonte's sweet-ness before. And now was not the suitable moment to tell his gentle hostess, that the time of the "negro" had long passed. He felt that he should permit himself that much black pride—indeed, he simply had to insist proudly, regardless of the condition of his bubbling guts.

Just then the bells of churches, near and far, began to fall into a joyful confusion of high and low ringing. Moody would have loved to hear how the Germans sing their hymns and carols. And in this moment he would have loved to thank the Lord Jesus for this evening. At least amongst his own folks this is how it was done. Amen.

Flannegan stood up and cleared his throat. He must have learned the speech by heart without really knowing what he was saying. Both hosts seemed amused.

And while Moody continued to applaud, Flannegen handed over his presents to the lady and to Justus. The packaging looked all too familiar to Moody. Identical or even his own? What if Flannegan had strictly followed the recommendations on the leaflet Instructions for soldiers in German families? Already, Moody was condemned to take the role of a clueless imitator. And so he heard as he had handed over his present, "Oh, handkerchiefs too! Very nice, really . . ."

The old lady had thought of something very special, real silk ties from her husband's wardrobe, too fine to be thrown away. One of each: plain, striped and plaid.

Justus filled the wineglasses on the table and carried them over to the tree, saying "Let's have some more Naked Ass!" He packed Belafonte away and swaying back and forth, put a 45 on the record player.

"Everybody! I wanna get up and do my thing!" came roaring from the loudspeakers. Justus grabbed Flannegan by the wrists and pulled him to the parquet in the center of the living room.

„Like a sex machine!" Justus screamed along with James Brown. "One, two, three, four!" Typical of average white folks, he had started his move on the beat, instead of off. He tried to stumble his way back into the rhythm while pulling Flannegan closer, but the officer extricated himself cleverly and claimed to have to visit the bathroom. Their hostess called for the maid and sent her to turn off the stereo. During her attempt to stop the music, she let the needle slip and a loud scratch cut through the vinyl.

Getting increasingly drunk, Justus accused his grand-mother of cultural ignorance, expecting full support from Moody.

"It was the negro who gave the blues to America!" Justus exclaimed passionately. Not quite right, Moody thought. It was America that gave the blues to the ‚negro‘, as Flip Wilson had said wittily.

By the time desert came around, the fun had been spoiled. The older woman looked exhausted, even though she tried to keep a smile on her face. Everyone ate their vanilla ice cream with chocolate sauce, the first dish that did not have a sour taste to it. Nervously, Justus sighed and glanced toward the hallway as Flannegan's portion began to melt away. Justus got up to see after the guest.

Lost in thought, the old woman used her spoon to draw fine, thin lines in the cream at the bottom of her desert bowl. Moody's presence didn't seem to interest her anymore. Politely, yet noticeably she observed the time displayed by the floor clock near the fireplace. A slight yawn emerged from behind her upheld hand.

It's the ice cream, he realized. He should have skipped the desert! His stomach had long been unwilling to accept too much foreign food in one sitting. His guts had turned sour and were ready for revenge. The first spasms proclaimed their resistance. Moody had to run if he wanted to reach the bathroom in time. With three, maybe four long jumps and a napkin in front of his mouth he reached the bathroom door and pulled it open. The grandson's tongue was sliding into the lieutenant's mouth and moved lustfully. Its lethargic counterpart awakened and adopted its movement to the rhythm of the strokes with which Justus raised the mast in Flannegan's pants.

His eyes wanted to turn away, but his stomach deman-ded a bucket or a bowl. Before Moody could decide his intestines demanded to be relieved, thereby unloading heavily over his pants and the shoes of the entwined couple. He stumbled past the dumbfounded lady, tore his coat from the hanger, and gave her a short sigh of apology: "Sorry." and was gone.

"You ungrateful negro, you!"

* * *

V

The icy air felt good, refreshing, even though his toes started to freeze after only a few steps through the snow. He was by himself. Or was he lonely? Mankind had withdrawn into their living rooms. Those who were outside, did not belong anywhere. Each cosily lit window promised a piece of happiness, but the spasms of his guts reminded him of the reality he had just faced— gluttony and fornication! Amen! He drifted towards the old part of the city, and listened to the singing coming from a nearby church. There was no feeling in it—it was monotonous, without the joy expressed by a touched heart and no fire burning in the singers' chests. How he would love to raise his voice and praise the Lord right then. Amen!

Some kids hanging out in one of the narrow alleys by the castle heard his singing.

"Cool, man!"

The snowfall was still and cold. In front of a pub, two muscled men in leather vests were arguing. Moody moved aside in order to avoid them. But, they had already noticed him and were calling, "Hey, man, come here, man!"

In broken English they invited him to come inside for a drink. It was Christmas after all and they needed his help. For only a moment. He was just in time, they said, and he might even make the newspapers if he was willing. Shuffled to the entrance Moody stopped to read the sign on the wall.

OFF LIMITS.

It basically meant the same as WHITES ONLY. Who the fuck did these Germans think they were? Even at home no damned redneck could prevent him from going anywhere if he wanted to. The guys kept pushing him, ignoring the sign. "Zzat bullshit, okay? Bullshit! Come on!"

His fingers ached from the cold. He wiped his runny nose with his sleeve. Warming up, that would do him good; it would calm him down. A big-bellied, mustached bartender welcomed him as if he had been a regular there for years. The bartender pushed a full beer mug across the bar and motioned for him to take a seat on the stool right by the window. Some other guests had already begun to watch suspiciously.

The two men had already stepped outside again and stood with their backs to the door of the bar. What a fool he must have been! Was he that drunk? The men wore vests with the emblem of a motorcycle gang: Heaven's Own. Still thrilled and blinded by all the Christmas glamor he'd had himself fooled by the fake friendliness of the two standing outside.

"I should have known better," he said to himself. Never in his life would he have fallen for such an ploy at home—it could cost him his life. Well, he thought, Germany was not Louisiana, and a bar in Aschaffenburg was not some KKK head-quarters—so he'd put his mind to rest.

"What's the blacky doing in here?" asked a skinny guy, who'd flung himself onto the stool right next to him. His leather vest left his biceps uncovered. On the right, the Rebel flag was twitching, the motto of the South tattooed: noli me tangere. Under his eyelids, tears of blue ink were etched indelibly, identifying him as someone who had done time.

Moody heard a voice say, "Leave him alone."

Amongst this herd of men the woman stood out like an Amazon as she walked over to the barkeep. Her words seemed to weigh heavily, as heavy as the silver jewelry with the turquoise stones she wore around her neck and arms. The color of her skin united all kinds of human conditions, a mixture of copper and olive. Black curls rested upon her shoulders. A narrow, elegant nose dominated her face, and her eyes seemed to look through everything and everybody. Moody needed some time before he was able to resist her glance, almost like the time it takes to get used to bright daylight once you awaken from a dream, especially when it was a dream as dark as the one that Moody felt caught himself in.

"When you leave them alone," the Amazon said, "they won't bother you—they're harmless then."

On each finger she wore an artfully designed silver ring with stones that looked like they had been mined from the American Southwest. And while Moody watched her draughting the beers, all attention went to the entrance. Lights flashed through the window. Two military police officers in white helmets entered the pub, followed by a group of men led by an elegantly dressed man.

"The Lord Mayor himself," Moody heard the Amazon say, while she refreshed the foam on the beer glasses.

Moody knew the colonel who was accompanying the city chief. It was Colonel Bacon the US military community commander, whose adjutant had just made him aware of the tipsy private sitting on a stool by the window. Something must have gone wrong. And it had to do with him. A man with a camera came up to him and asked him his name, taking notes. "Moody—I mean Rufus Moody, Junior."

The leaders seemed horrified by the situation they found themselves in and after a short conference they decided to leave, anger on their faces. A moment later the Colonel's adjutant returned. Furiously the major explained how this joint action was meant to catch the pub owner by surprise and to accuse him of discrimination by declaring his place off limits to American soldiers.

„Especially blacks," he added on. Tonight they even had the local press on their side.

"We could have solved this problem once and for all. And here you sit, you— the colonel is pissed off, I can't tell how much, soldier. You will report to your company commander first thing in the morning, in uniform, as clean as a baby's butt, you hear? Now, get out of here!"

The major was right, Moody thought, as he discovered the puke on his shoes. He felt his guts welling up and felt disgust at his own appearance.

"The blacky smells bad, time to go." The skinny tattooed guy came creeping up again. The Amazon had disappeared. Well it surely was time to go, the bartender agreed, with a conciliating nod of his head.

A bit of black pride was needed now. Stand! Moody told himself. He ordered another beer, but his request was ignored. The tattooed guy turned friendly and explained that the Germans would like to be by themselves at least this one night—on Christmas. "Can you understand that?" he asked Moody.

Moody turned to face and him asked, "Are you talking about real Germans, those who have German mothers?

That was exactly what he meant, the guy replied. Moody slid off of his stool and stood in front of the tattoed man.

"Let me tell you something, you little son of a bitch—my mother is Gabi from Versbach, and she is ten times more a German mother than yours and your motherfucking daddy altogether. Who's your daddy, do you know? Some Polack, some Italian scumbag?"

Men in black leather vests surrounded him. The bartender pushed through the ring of bodies. "Go! Out, now!"

"There's gotta be at least a bit of pride, you understand, man?" Moody wanted to pay for his drink, but the barkeep didn't want to be bothered. "No, just get out!"

"No, man, I'm gonna pay my bill!"

The gang held still.

Moody fumbled for his wallet. Empty. Nothing—he had given it all to Winslow on Jackson's behalf. He started to grin madly.

"Just go now, okay?" The Amazon had returned and made way for him through the excited crowd. At the exit she saw to it that no one followed him.

Wilder than before, the wind whipped the snow through the alley. Where to? Instinctively, Moody chose the way back to the barracks, but only went as far as the park that separated the inner city from the military quarters. He trotted along a path which led along a frozen lake. He slowly came to realize that it might not have been such a good idea after all to meet up with his German half-brothers. He seemed to be the only one who felt incomplete without revitalizing his German roots—the lacking half of his identity.

From a shack in the center of the park he heard a sheep bleating. Approaching the structure, Moody could see there was a door that was only secured by a loose pawling—easy to squeeze through. The door could be closed from the inside, locking out the cold wind. Three sheep huddled in a straw-covered corner.

The shadow of two large statues should have shocked him; but they looked so familiar that immediately the words of the angel came to mind: "Do not be afraid. I bring you good news of great joy for all the people."

Between the figures stood a crib, where a wood-carved figure of the infant Jesus lay, smiling at him. Moody joined the Holy Family, sitting on a bale of straw. The scent of the sheep was sharp, but they stared at him, accepting him as one of their own—a black sheep, however. And they allowed him to warm his hands in their woolen coats.

"It's me y'all, the third king," he said to the child and pulled the peacemaker from his shirt. "I bring you the incense."

From his trouser pocket he produced the box of matches with the angel's picture, that the maid had given him. He struck a match and led it to the tip of the joint, setting it aglow.

Moody breathed in deeply, the bitter smoke mixing with the animal scent of the stall. Silent, with every draw he grew calmer—able to produce pictures and memories from within himself, thoughts of Gabi from Versbach, who he would find soon—thoughts of the old woman to whom he owed an apology as good manners were customary to his people. He saw the guys in the Kaserne fussin' and fightin', and saw Uncle Sly waving at him from over a heaving sea of bamboo spears. The angel on the match box spread its wings. And while Rufus Moody, Jr. closed his eyes, the cherub transformed into the shape of Curtis Mayfield lifting his voice:

Little child - runnin' wild
Watch a while - you see he never smiles

Moody dropped the roach into the crib, where its glow lit up the straw.

In the back of his mind he's sayin'
Didn't have to be here
You didn't have to love for me
While I was just a nothin' child
Why couldn't they just let me be?

Let me be, let me be, let me be ...

- End -

Quotes from „Freddie's Dead" and "Little Child Runnin' Wild" are taken from the Album "Superfly" by Curtis Mayfield, 1972